The Madre and Gander Employment Agency
David Macpherson

1. The Table Settings Ran Away

It was my third job interview of the day. I was yelled at by the first firm, because I wiped my nose with a tissue and not a handkerchief. The second interview forgot I was coming. They made me wait a half hour until they found someone to look at my resume and ask four questions. I think the last question was, "Accountant, huh? So you like numbers?

Walking into the third possible job, The Madre and Gander Employment Agency, there was no denying that I felt terrible. Like I was useless and unwanted. Like I was a rodent, just vermin. With that in mind, when I walked into my third interview, I was greeted by three cats standing on the reception desk shouting at each other.

"That's not a fiddle."

"Please, I am too sophisticated to call my instrument such a word. It is a violin."

"But that isn't even a violin. That's a ukulele with a bow."

"Yes, we sophisticated animals like to call that a violin."

"And we rubes and headcases know that that is nothing of the sort. That's why we call it a ukelele with a bow, because it is."

"How uneducated you are."

"Let's ask this guy. The pale skinny guy. Let's ask him. He can judge. What is that thing the short tabby is holding?"

I have been asked many out of left field questions during a job interview, but this one might have been the most nerve inducing. "Do I need to answer?"

One of the cats raised up his hands in victory, "Ukulele it is!"

At that moment, a small, wrinkly woman smelling of mothballs barreled out of a door in the back. "Talent should not be bothering the public! You squawkers should know not to hassle a nice young boychik coming in. Probably by accident too, I shouldn't be surprised."

"Squawkers! We are artists!"

"Yeah, cat artists!"

"Leave the little thing alone, you're frightening him. I'm not going to give out any jobs to overgrown kittens who scare the public. Now quiet down and let the non-talent folk talk," she glared at the cats and they leaped off the desk and went to the benches and sat down. "That's better."

She glared at me. "Boychick, you know better to bother these flea bitten thespians. Didn't mother tell you, don't talk to money lenders or feline actors? No? What's happening to mothers these days?"

I winced backwards. This was turning into the shortest and worst of the day's three interviews. Why couldn't I just get a nice dull job at a place that money launders for the mob? They must be calmer and more organized than anything I had come across yet. "I just want a bookkeeping job. I just want to look at spreadsheets. I just want to clock in and fill in forms and not talk to people or cats or, wait, is that walking silverware?"

I raised my hand and pointed with a shaky finger at a small group of utensils with faces and limbs walking through the door. The old woman followed my direction and snorted. "That's not silverware. Don't flatter those reprobates. You might go as far as saying they are cutlery, but that even is too good for them, that's for certain. Those are damned spoons. Spoons that missed their appointment time by two hours. Sheers should be put to them, making them sporks for all the good they are."

One of the spoons, with rosy cheeks of all things, put up his hands, "Now Ethel, you don't have to be so mean there. Are we a little late? Perhaps. Maybe we were working another gig for you and had no choice but to be late."

"And maybe you were at Grimms having morning boilermakers as a pick me up," the woman who I supposed was Ethel said. She leaned in close to the spoon and said, "Let me see your eyes. Yeah, they are slightly tarnished. You and your set are soused. You should leave my respectable establishment and get a job as skidrow catapults."

"You don't have to be so rude, Ethel. You are not the only agency in town."

"Then go to them. With my blessing. And being that no one in the business likes me one whit, my blessing is worth not even a kopek. Besides, I already hired a spoon and a dish for the gig. These folk came on time." Ethel made a shooing gesture with her hand and turned her back. The spoons looked at each other, shrugged, or did as close to a shrug as silverware can, and left.

She turned her head to me. "Are they gone?" she asked me in a poor stage whisper.

"The spoons? Yes. The cats are still here."

"That's cats for you," she said. "Besides, I'm still hiring for cats. There is always something for cats in this business, but you know how it is." She gave me a conspiratorial wink.

I nearly wept. "No. I do not know what you mean. Not one bit."

She looked at me like she was trying to find out if my eyes were tarnished as well. "You came for the bookkeeping job? You are hired. You survived coming through the door. That is all you need to work here. Actually, you need a lot more than that, but who said the key to success was showing up?"

She paused and looked at me, waiting for an answer. "Is that something I should know? I don't know who said it. I'm sorry. Did I, well, am I going to, I mean, do I need to know who said that."

She patted my head, "The right answer to that, boychik, from now on, for your best reference, is that I said it. Me, Ethel. Others might have warbled it out before me, but I am the only one who meant it like I do. Whoah, this is the longest job interview in the history of hiring practice. You're wearing me out kid and I desperately need another cigarette. Naturally, I always want another cigarette. That's the joy of those little tobacco filled delights, you just want another. Like rugelach, who can have just one. Ah, rugelach. I finish one of those little beauts and there I am wanting another. Where was I?"

"You were I think hiring me or planning on having a cigarette or maybe eating something that probably tastes delicious but sounds like you were just clearing your throat, but I think you were going to hire me for a job."

"Mostly, planning on a cigarette, but yeah, sure. Boychik, you know your numbers?"

"Sure, I wouldn't take the job if I didn't."

"Don't get ruffled feathers, I am not hiring for the goose that laid the golden egg today, thank goodness. Having a room filled with fowl is annoying because no matter what time of year it is, they are always molting."

I knew I should have been relieved about the job, but I felt even more squeezed. "What would be my role?"

"Cinnamon." She squinted at me, looking for a reaction. "That was a joke. Some good it did for your pallor. Relax, kid. You got a good paying job. I have your resume. I think. If I looked at it, I am sure it was adequate. We are looking for basic accounts payable and payroll. We take the money in from the clients and pay our talent from that. No withholdings for them, actors. They should give us money for the tumult they cause."

"What kind of business is this?" I craned around unsure of what I was seeing.

"We are a casting agency, my little pet. We supply both featured and walk-on roles for fairy tales, folk tales and the occasional shaggy dog story. If someone wants a new Red Riding Hood story they can call us up and we get them what they want. Today, we had calls for two new productions of Hey Diddle Diddle. Hey Diddle Diddle, that's a dirty joke waiting to be said. But the kiddies love it. Or the adults who make this drivel think the kiddies love it. Don't matter to me or my sister none, we get work for our talent which means money for us."

"You do this with your sister? Is she Madre or Gander?"

She slapped her forehead. "Kid, you work here, I want you to balance the books but good, but you also have to figure out a sense of humor. My sister is Bea, Beatrice. She is the good witch. Me? Not so much. But I am a generous boss, at least. I ain't paying the moon, but you ain't going to go hungry. You in?"

"I think I should say, let me think of it? I think that's what I should say."

She presented a thin but wide grin. "You should say, I have to run out of this place as fast as I can and never come back, I should catch up with the dish and the spoon and run to the safest breakfast hutch I can find. That's what you should say. But what you are going to do is take off your coat, drape it on this chair, because I don't have a coat rack, why bother in a place like this. And then you will go to the break room and make a pot of coffee, I make paint thinner every time I attempt such a task. Now remember, when you set up the coffee, we don't have spoons, but swizzle sticks. We hire out spoons, even drunk nogoodnik ones, and it would not be right to also have them stir our morning joe, would it?"

I felt faint. "Wait. I'm starting now? I'm making coffee? I'm respecting the talking spoons by not using them in my everyday life? Did I even say I would take the job?"

She looked at me. "What's your name boychik?"

"Tony."

"Tony, you are hired whether you like it or not. Give it six months. You will love it"

I took off my coat without thinking and said, "How do you know that for certain?"

"Because, boychik, you're in show business now."

2. Had a Great Fall

I don't know, but every now and again, there is a rush in a certain kind of character. That's when we go from an empty office, with the phone dead and silent, to a waiting area teaming life and livestock. And not just packed but packed with all of the same character to place. Like an office full of Hansel and Gretels. Just imagine small little german kids in lederhosen bumping into the furniture and going on about how hungry they are. Ethel calls it a Character Mob.

There was that time that I couldn't get in the door from the crush of Bo Peeps everywhere. They were all there for a mattress commercial gig. The idea being that the reason she can't find her sheep is that all of those furry little devils are jumping over the beds at this mattress store. And if the sheep like it, then you will want to buy one too. Yeah, it didn't sound like a great concept to me either, but when do you ever come across a clever commercial?

There was not a lot of call for blonde women in pinafores calling out for livestock at that time, so everyone of them was there at Madre and Gander Employment Agency. Of course, they weren't looking for absconded sheep, but the ever elusive paycheck. With that said, they all appeared a little desperate.

It wouldn't have been so bad if there wasn't all those shepherding staffs tripping me up. I was slapped four times from Bo Peeps thinking I was getting fresh instead of just losing my balance. One shouted at me, "Hey buddy, I lost my sheep, not my self respect. Watch it why dontcha?" I was mortified. I don't see myself as a handsy kind of guy. As a bookkeeper, I'm into numbers, but not into figures, if you get my meaning. Sorry, I'm also not a good comic, but you should have already realized that by now. "Excuse me Madame," I said, and that got them all madder.

It was not a good way to start a morning.

But being assaulted by put upon shepherdesses, was not as uncomfortable as the day we were hiring for three different Humpty Dumpty jobs. We had thirty or more giant egg men in the waiting area at the front of the shop. Scary group of people, if you ask me. But it wasn't the ovoid bodies and anachronous waist coats that made it so unsettling. It was the puns.

All of them were cracking puns.

See? Cracking. Cracking puns. That was one that they said. There were derivations to this "joke."

-You crack me up

-You're cracked

-Crack open another

You get the idea. After a dozen of crack puns, one of the Humptys threw his tiny hands over his eyes, or at least tried to because his arms were not long enough, and exclaimed, "That's un oeuf of that." The Humpty looked at me staring at him and said, "I said it because it sounds like enough but really I said, un oeuf, which is how the French say an egg. Get it? Un oeuf. I'm an egg. Enough. It's funny."

Another Humpty laughed at him and said, "Yeah, you can tell how funny it was to him by how much he is laughing, which is not at all. So I guess the yolks on you."

Another joined in, "Yeah, your sense of humor surely was mis-laid."

"Stop jostling, there are too many of you here, what if there is a fire, no one would be able to get to the eggs-it."

"Oh I would be the first one out of here in an emergency, I can really scramble."

"Of course you would think that because you are an egg-o-maniac."

I pushed my fingers into my ears as tightly as possible and ran into Ethel's office and shut the door. "Save me from the bad egg puns," I pleaded.

Ethel ground out her cigarette and slowly looked up at me. She had an expression of puzzlement that made me wonder if she even knew who I was. "Tony. Tony. Oh hey. How are you. I'm just waiting out the inevitable here. How goes it?" She waved me to a chair, which I didn't take because of the three feet of file folders teetering on it like a tower in Pisa.

I leaned against the door, just in case any of the Humpties attempted to enter. "The puns. The waiting area is filled with puns."

She gave me another puzzled look. "No. There are no puns out there. I checked. What we got out there is a bunch of eggs. Big ugly eggs. When you watch them talk, doesn't it kind of give you the shivering heebies? I know it does for me. I don't like it when we have to hire talking food. Inanimate objects, like dishes running off with spoons or any other cutlery, that's fine. But when we got food products having faces and talking, I don't know, that's when this job gets kind of hard."

"And they're telling puns," I said again. "This is something that should be considered and addressed as soon as possible. There are awful egg puns going on. Can you just hire the Humpty that you peg is right for the ad or whatever they are needed for and send the rest away?"

"I'm just waiting for the inevitable end to occur, Tony, and then I will do the selecting and we are off to the races. We get the right Humpty to the client and everyone is ecstatic." She lit another cigarette and leaned back in her chair, without a care or twitching nerve ending in the world.

"I can't sit out there and get any work done, Ethel. Not with all the yolks and the cracking and the French terms and everything. How can I balance a spreadsheet if I am hearing this?"

She suddenly leaned forward, jutted her head in my direction and pointed her lit cigarette at me, as if to make her point apparently clear. "Let me ask you something Tony. This is not me changing the subject or being clever with subterfuge. This is me asking the most pertinent question of the day. You ready? You ready to have me, blow your mind? That's the expression, right? Blow your mind? Mind blown? That's right, isn't it?"

I exhaled a surrendering sigh, "Okay, shoot. What pertinent question is going to blow my mind?"

"Alright then, what is Humpty Dumpty? Just use the text, the information the poem gives you. What is Humpty Dumpty?"

I looked at her, unsure that that was the mind blowing question she really wanted to toss at me. "Are you kidding, Ethel? It's Humpty Dumpty. We got more than a score of them out there. You can hear them now with the puns and the talking and the one upmanship. The damned Humpties. They're eggs. Big anthropomorphic, scary looking eggs."

Ethel gave me a smile like she only now awarded the crown for the best fairy tale casting agent prize. "Really? Why do you say that?"

"Come on Ethel. Look at any book or cartoon or commercial. There is Humpty Dumpty. And he's an egg. A big horrendous, nightmare inducing egg. But he's an egg."

"Ah-ha. Pictures. You are bringing up pictures. But the words. The words don't say anything about being an egg. Does it? It's been a long time since I have sat down to give a rousing recitation of the Humpty Dumpty epic, but I am pretty sure that the words egg, yolk, shell, or even omelet are not in the telling."

I was silent for a moment. I recited the poem in my head. I did it again. I slowed it down and even moved my lips as I rediscovered that poem like for the first time. "There is no egg in the poem."

"Of course there is no egg in the poem or on my face, for that matter," Ethel said, pleased. "According to some dull, boring history fella, Humpty Dumpty was the name of a type of cannon that was bolted to the side of a castle. I guess this cannon fell and the king's horses and men couldn't fix it. Maybe they lost the user's manual. But who wants to have a fairy tale character that's nothing but a piece of armament? It doesn't sell coloring books or plushy toys."

"How did it become an egg, then?"

"Who knows. My guess is that some hungry talent agent had him a giant egg as a client but with no prospects for booking him for any kind of a job. So this hypothetical talent agent thought about it and found this little nursery rhyme property and marketed that Humpty Dumpty was a giant egg man. He probably paid off a writer to make Humpty be that way, like that weird Alice in Wonderland writer. His palm got greased, no doubt and he wrote what was supposed to be a wall mounted cannon into an egg with eyes and ears. Such ears those eggs have. After a while, producers wanted to book the new Humpty Dumpty incarnation, and that was what the talent agent was waiting for. Because he had the only humanoid egg in the registry. Hey presto and just like that, Humpty Dumpty is an egg."

I shook my head. I was only her employee for a few months, but I knew better than believing her story. "Do you even believe that yourself?"

"Who knows, Tony. You asked me how it could happen, and I gave what I think is the most logical explanation. It's an egg because it looks good on the screen or in magazine ads. Actually, when I was a little girl, growing up wherever I grew up, I can't ever be sure where that was. There was a subway stop near where we lived, so I can rule out Atlantis, at least. Anyway, when I was a little girl, Humpty Dumpty wasn't a cannon or an egg. In my neighborhood, Humpty Dumpty was a blintz. Sometimes he had lemon filling, sometimes it was blueberry. What a self respecting blintz was doing hanging out on a wall was always a mystery, but I'm sure you can ask the same thing about a giant egg on a wall too."

"What's a blintz?"

"A blintz you don't know?" She seemed aghast for a second and then broke out into a knowing smile. "Of course you don't know. A blintz is the finest of deserts. It is a wonderfully fluffy pancake that is then wrapped around a filling like lemon custard or blueberry. Then you give a give dollop of powdered sugar on top and then you bite into heaven. Heaven I say. Why is it I say the word HoHo and you know what that is."

"It's what Santa Claus says sliding down a chimney," I piped in.

"Let's not mention the Christmas Elf, shall we," Ethel spat. "We are having nice conversations while keeping ourselves away from punning eggs. Why bring up that ruffian? No I say HoHo and you think of a food perhaps."

"Oh that's the Hostess cake with the cream filling and the chocolate coating. Good stuff."

She harumphed. "Good stuff he says. Good stuff. This you know. A blintz? It's a mystery. A puzzle. A blintz was what we ate during special days, Oh it was good. And when we told stories of Humpty Dumpty, that's what he was. A giant blintz with a face and dangling arms and legs that didn't seem to fit the requirements of the body.

"When the great fall happened, the fall broke him into ripped pieces and the filling splattering all over the kingsmen and the horses. Nothing funnier than a king's horse covered in lemon custard." She leaned on her hands and smiled a sleepy, far-away grin.

I stood wondering why I was there. Then I remembered. We were escaping all the punning. But, I wasn't hearing any punning from the other room. As a matter of fact, I wasn't hearing anything. The sudden quiet threw me off, though it took a while for me to figure it out. "Hey, Ethel. They finally got wise, all those Humpties. They are now quietly waiting for you to cast them."

"Oh no, Tony. They are not quietly waiting. They are probably all cracked and scrambled. The puns turned to fisticuffs and fisticuffs and giant humanoid eggs don't mix too well."

I turned to the door and edged it open. I saw only one Humpty Dumpty standing by himself. He was gasping for breath and covered in egg yolk. Somebody else's egg yolk. This was no self inflicted wound!

I looked and the waiting area was a jungle of cracked, jagged egg shells. There were egg shells stuck to the walls. Some of the broken shells had the impression of a nose, or a mouth or the impression of a furrowed brow.

I guess it would have been acceptable, well almost acceptable, if it wasn't for the yellow yolk splatter patterns everywhere. There were also areas where the egg white was frothed up from all the tussling that must have happened. So some corners were whipped up like a merengue. It was a slaughter. It was a ham fisted drunken cooking night. And everything that could be beaten was.

Ethel didn't seem to notice the carnage. She walked over to the one remaining Humpty and said, "You know what son. You have the look we are searching for. You are most definitely the best egg for the shoot."

The Humpty, still covered in egg viscera, looked practically shocked. "Really? I have the part?"

"Now, it's not a big role. It's in a dream sequence where the main character isn't sure of a decision he made. You are there as a visual prompt to do the right thing. Let me call the director, and inform him that we are sending you for the gig tomorrow, seven sharpish. And for goodness sakes, boychik, clean yourself up. You're a sight."

The Humpty jumped up to high five someone, but being that everyone was shattered, he only leapt up with his arm up, as if he had an important question to ask the teacher.

Ethel went into her office and I followed. "We have a yolky massacre out there." I stated. "And you are congratulating the sole survivor with a job."

"Of course Tony. It happens every time. They tell puns until they attack each other, because that's the logical conclusion to punning, mass destruction. The final Humpty deserves the job, and I don't have to audition them and figure out which humanoid egg is better than all the other humanoid eggs. Who can decide that? They are all so creepy."

"What about the mess?" I asked.

Ethel chuckled. "The mess. Go into Bea's rolodex and get to the C's. Call up some of the Cinderellas we have. Those girls know their way around a broom and a mop. Tell them if they do a good job, we might be able to hook them up with a possible Shoe commercial account."

3. Slow and Steady

The waiting area was teaming with furry woodland critters. The place had more of the appearance of the adorable than I can ever recall. You have to travel pretty far and wide to come across a more cuddly employment agency then our little shingle this particular afternoon.

The gig that we were hiring for was a new version of a Christmas Carol where all the players were animals; the cuter and more cloying the better. Bea was always in charge of the accounts that recast classics of literature with animals. It was a special gift for her. Give her a classic text, any classic text, and she could menagerie it. Show her Robinson Crusoe, say, and in Bea's liver spotted hands, you might get a survival tale of guinea pigs, and you would love it. The way she was able to cast a production of Don Quixote with salamanders is still talked about. It wasn't just cute, it was profound. I can't even see a picture of a windmill without thinking of that misguided little fire lizard and become teary.

Now for this Christmas Carol, the production company took care of casting the main characters. We were tasked with the extras. I'm sure Bea was a little put out with that. Her stamp on an animal Scrooge and Marley had to be better than the dog and cat the producers cast. Scrooge as a pooch, who hasn't seen that?

We had the nameless characters, the background color. Our waiting area was packed with the precious. All the poor urchins must be cute and pettable. I was having a difficult time focusing on processing the accounts payables when all I wanted to do was cuddle with our clients.

I noticed a lean bunny rabbit leaning up against a bench, rolling a toothpick around his teeth. Now that was not a cute activity, and I figured that if I wanted to get back to work anytime soon, it was this type of thing I should be focusing on. This rabbit possessed the rapt attention of a couple chipmunks and a spiky haired vole.

The rabbit chuckled and said, "Yeah. This background work is good for me. I mean, I can be a lead actor easy. It's in my blood. I can be any of the ghosts of Christmas and these yahoo producers would thank me all day till Sunday for me agreeing to it. I ain't bragging. I ain't telling stories. I am a bunny with pedigree. My great grandfather was the Easter Bunny for a few years. And he wasn't fired like some ducks are saying. Can't trust waterfowl, they are jealous and lie. That's just the truth. Ducks are mean customers.

"My great granddad decided that Easter was not good enough for him and he ran in the general election to be the new spokesmodel for Christmas. It goes without saying that the fix was in. Santa won again, he always wins. You got to wonder about that, how does he always win the slot year in and year out? How can that be without a little juice flowing? Well the answer is, it can't. The jolly little elf is just the guy the machine picked to be its front man. A shame, because what the holidays needs is a fleet footed rabbit who can really be fast in delivering presents and candy and what not.

"And that wasn't the only one in my family tree worth talking about. My Uncle Andy, for example, was the rabbit who lost the race with the turtle. That's a great story and I get hired to do remakes of that one all the time. I take great pride when I get booked for one of those gigs. I alway pour a little bit of my Hard Carrot Juice on the ground to pay respect to that great progenitor. The man who threw the race.

"What? Do you really think he actually fell asleep near the end of the race because he was so cocky? Nah. My Uncle Andy was a businessman. He put all his money on the turtle. Now the Vegas line was heavy for Uncle Andy. I think the line was 78 to 3. That's not a lot of money to make, but the whole family bankrolled Andy with their life savings and he was able to find a bookie, who was Mama Bear. Yeah, Papa Bear and Baby Bear, didn't know it, but the old lady ursine was making book and the little blondie girl was her runner. The reason that Goldilocks ruined the house in that story you heard of was not a simple case of B and E but a case of getting the day's bets and dispersing the paper.

"But Goldilocks was not working that day. The bet was placed directly with Mama Bear. They found a drunk strung out porcupine to play patsy and pay the Bear.

"The race happened and Uncle Andy attempted to keep the event tight, only running at quarter speed. That was the plan, but he's a rabbit. A rabbit with legs and pride. He had to go fast. He had to whip through that course. How could he not? Is grass not to be green and smokable? Did I mention that Uncle Andy was pretty high at the time? A kite, he was high. So he was flying and enjoying the run and the turtle was way behind.

"Then the panic came in when he saw the finish line approaching. So he just slammed the breaks and pretended to be asleep. He couldn't think of any other ruse. He was out of good ideas, so he picked the first one that came to him.

"The turtle sludged past him and he pretended to wake up and speed to the finish line, only to come up photo finish short. Just like he intended all along.

"That was my uncle, he was famous because of that. Didn't make a dime though. Mama Bear knew that he threw the race. I mean, really. Fell asleep in the middle? Who ever falls asleep in the middle when there is money to be had? Mama Bear found the patsy, the drunk porcupine, and plucked out quills until he gave up Uncle Andy. Mama Bear was never one to waste anything, but showed her dissatisfaction by returning the pulled out quills, not back to Porcupine but into Uncle Andy. Poor Andy, he looked like an unfinished connect the dot activity page. He never got the money and he is now known as being one of the laziest athletes in all of history.

"But my point, my little friends. is that he is known. There are a lot more successful woodland characters who are not dragged out and reenacted. He was stabbed by quills, but he is still a go to character. Hell, I even played him in a couple of Saturday morning cartoons. I did my uncle proud."

One of the voles listening blew a raspberry, which I am sorry to say, was also damned adorable. The rabbit's eyes widened "I'm sorry," he said to the vole, "if I offended you with my heartfelt story of my family. I didn't realize that personal stories are to be ridiculed."

The vole squeaked up, "I'm not calling BS on heartfelt family sagas. I'm just calling BS on your family saga. I mean, let's look at the timeline you got here. The tortoise and the hare story is, what? Two thousand years old? How can your Uncle be in that old old story."

The rabbit laughed, "Oh, I see the confusion now. You are just a bit turned around. This is easily explained. This old story you are talking about, what's the name? Tortoise and the Hare? Well I don't know anything about that story. That could very well be two thousand years old. But the story my Uncle Andy was in was called The Rabbit and the Turtle's Big Time Race. Totally different."

The vole shook his head. "I call BS on that too. Sorry, but whatever you call it, it's still the same story that has been dinging around for longer than your family has."

The rabbit put up a paw, "You don't understand time, of course it's my family and of course it is as old as it needs to be. You gotta trust the story. The story you know and the story I'm telling. Compare the two? Which one will you trust more? Which one is more fun to listen to?"

"Neither," the vole stated, "they are both simple minded pedantic object lessons with a poor plot device wedged into the end to justify the moral."

"I don't know what you are going on about, friend vole. Just know that my family is a lucky one and I am sure to get a good role in this Christmas Carol."

I wish to say that he didn't get the job. But they all did. They were all furry and worked for below scale (Bea had a deal with the union to underpay woodland performers). The rabbit was all smug about it. "Told you I would get the job. In the bag," he bragged to anyone around to hear.

Without thinking, I grabbed this rabbit up and petted him until I was satisfied and he was mortified. It was the least I could do.

4. Ethel on the Phone

All of it? You shaved off all of it? Did you go somewhere? No, not to a bar. To a barber! Did you get it shaved off professionally? Yourself? You shaved off all that hair by yourself? Where is it? What do you mean what do I mean? Where is the hair? That was a lot of hair you removed from your scalp, kiddo. It's in the back bedroom? You put your hair in the back room? Why did you put it in the back room? Wait. Stop. Never mind. Don't tell me. No good will come to me for knowing how your mind and its concept of logic works. If I listen to your logic, I might wind up shaving off all of my hair.

No, no. That is not a good idea. I like my hair. I like the blue rinse and the way the sun hits it. I am a lady of a certain age and I like being blue haired and I don't shave my head. And if I was the type to do so, it would be better than you doing it?

Why? She asks me why? This is the question she comes up with? She doesn't come up with the question of should a woman booked for a three day commercial shoot as Rapunzel shave off all her hair after only the first day of the booking? Does that question not occur to you? It should.

Why is that bad? Why is that bad? Kiddo, you should lay off the why questions. They don't do my digestion any good. I am burping up the tongue sandwich I had three hours ago. Why is that bad? Because you can't go back tomorrow to the set and take off your baseball cap to reveal to the hair and makeup people that you are bald!

No. No, there is nothing wrong with a woman being bald. Well, actually, it's not a look I care for, but that's not the point. There is nothing wrong with that if, say you are working as a seamstress in a seventh floor walk up sweatshop putting zippers in knock-off designer jeans and you come in without a follicle on your pate. That's fine. It probably is a smart move with working in such a hot airless place.

But you are not a seamstress. You are a skinny girl with really long hair. Scary long hair. You are a girl signed up with my agency to go out on

Rapunzel gigs. Perfect for a girl with insanely long locks. Not particularly ideal for a bald girl.

Yes, I know, the hair limits you. No Snow White or Little Mermaid work for a girl with tresses stretching to Southern New Jersey. You have to take only the Rapunzel bookings. For that reason, I don't have many Rapunzels in the Mail List. And that's by design, kiddo. I don't want a feeding frenzy for too few jobs. I keep only the best.

I only ask for two things. I want a client who picks up the phone on the second or third ring and does not say no. I want a girl with long hair who says, "A job next week? You bet." I need that "you bet" to be loud and clear and true. And I need them to have long hair.

Kiddo, kiddo. You don't have to tell me again. You told me. And believe me I heard. You shaved your hair. You no longer a trapped princess. You are now an unemployable actress calling from a cheap apartment that is now newly decorated with a large mound of discarded hair.

Don't be upset. Don't be surprised. No. Honey, no. Stop that right now, No. Don't go to the director. Do not tell him about the new edgy direction that he should take.

Dark and edgy is not something directors really want to do. They want to be called that. They want to have dark vision and edgy visuals, but really, they want to have the next job. They can call themselve dark and edgy, but really most directors are made of marshmallow fluff. You are part of a dream sequence sure, but that doesn't mean he wants a punk rock Rapunzel. He wants a basic Rapunzel in a basic tower being harried by a basic witch. The kind whose oversized nose has a wart on the end of it. Basic. Generic. Pretty girl in tower? Check. Ridiculous amount of blonde locks that can be used as a ladder? Check. Wait, not a check anymore.

No, kiddo, please. I don't want to hear the explanation. I don't need to. I know what you are going to say.

You could not stand being defined by your hair. You are a real woman with real feelings. But all anyone sees are the tresses. You start to think that you are nothing but hair. A big mess of hair with a nameless girl attached. You don't think of yourself as a feminist, per se, but you area determined individual nonetheless and this adoration of the hair is demeaning to all princesses and women alike. And it is not fair. There are balding women who strive for a good fairy tale gig, but can't. The public expects a pretty girl with crazy hair. They are selecting a dull world but refusing to explore the variety of life. Why couldn't Rapunzel be bald? Why couldn't the hair be armpit hair? You realize this is a gross thought, but that's only because you have been brainwashed by this pop culture miazma. You think that you will show them by cutting a little of the hair off and it shears off easy as butter. And then you shear off some more. And some still until you are bald and at first you are exultant but you realize that they expect you for a six AM call. Wait, they are not expecting you. They are expecting a Rapunzel like you find in the picture books. And that's not you anymore.

How do I know that? Do you think you are my first Rapunzel with a mad razor? You aren't even the fifth bald Rapunzel. And it's always the same. The second or third day of the gig and the regrets hit. Maybe I should book Rapunzels for one day shoots only. Could I do that?'

Probably not. You will be fine. Stop the crying. That does nothing but eat away at your complexion. Tears are more corrosive than acid rain. It's true. I heard it on a TV show somewhere. Now if I remember, the last time we had a Rapunzel sheering we were prepared. My sister Bea insisted that instead of an insurance rider, we buy a giant Rapunzel wig.

It's tawny blonde like yours. Not exactly like yours, but here's what you will do. I will send Tony to the storage unit and get the wig. He'll have to take the truck because that wig is huge. Why am I saying this part? Kiddo, Tony is eavesdropping as we speak and I figured I would tell him what he needs to do this evening.

He's going to drive to you and help fit it on you. You need to get to the set an hour early. I will call a hair stylist who works at that studio to meet you. She will dye that thing until it is the same color as your late lamented natural tresses. Just to touch it or play with it. Directors are known for their impeccable eye for detail, but that's baloney. They don't notice any of the important things. Like their long haired princess donning a clever wig. He won't even have a clue. Directors are easy marks.

You're welcome. Well, you are slightly forgiven, at least. I really wish this didn't happen, but it did. The artistic temperament.

Will I use you again? That's a question. You are off my list for Rapunzels. I can get you some wicked stepsister action. You can wear whatever crazy wig is necessary and you have proven to have a vein of madness. Directors love it. Not for princesses. But you can do the pretty but evil witch that almost sways the Charming. You know, there is a call for a sexed up Baba Yaga in a series of television movies. How's your Russian?

5. We Don't Do Christmas

I was working on the week's payables when a shadow blocked all light around my desk. There is always someone putting their shadow on my desk, but this one was something immense and kind of frightening. I looked up to see the looming body of a goat devil. He was seven feet tall, with the legs of a goat. He was a creature that was into body building. His face was triangular. There were horns and sharp teeth and a very pointy beard. "I have come to speak to Ethel for possible employment." He had a rich gravy voice that I might guess was German or something Teutonic, if I was to be pressed.

I gulped. "Is she expecting you?"

The large devil goat man thing laughed, "No, that Ethel is not expecting me. She might not be surprised that I turned up, but I am sure she is not expecting me."

"Would it work for me to say that she is very busy and cannot see you at this time?"

The large devil goat man thing laughed once more. He certainly was merry. "You," he said. "You are funny and I like you. You will go far. Great distances, I am sure. But right, all the distance you need to go is to the Ethel's door."

I went. I opened the door. Ethel was standing on her desk, writing nasty words on the ceiling tiles. "Don't bother me with my hobbies," she said. She turned around and saw the look on my face. "If what you are thinking is that you would like to go into the corner of Ethel's office and puke up all that sugar and traif you deign to eat all day, then you can turn around and just leave a poor dying woman alone."

"There is a devil who wants to see you," I stammered out.

"A devil, you say," she smiled slightly and jumped off the desk. "Now devils are not what we do. They are not completely what we are known for. But you know my sweet genteel Bea, she always wants to diversify our portfolio, whatever that might mean. So maybe if he is a cute little red devil with a pitchfork, such a dear. Let's give him a look."

Ethel bounded out of the office with determination. When she saw the devil waiting by my desk she stopped and swore. "Tony, boychik, that's not a devil. A devil is a fella that we can get behind. A devil is a money making concern because what ad campaign doesn't' love the frisky little devil? This is not the Devil. This is something much worse. This is a Krampus, kennahura."

I looked at Ethel and then spun myself to face the fellow with the goat's legs and the horns and the beard. "No," said I, "this is a devil."

"Well, yes, that's true. But it is also true that they come from the same source material but believe me, they are quite different. This is Krampus, the Christmas antagonist."

Krampus nodded enthusiastically. "Yes, I am he. I am the Krampus. The scourge of the yuletide. But I don't have to be. I can be just your average run of the mill devil. Your employee could be correct. I could be the best devil you ever had."

Ethel spat on the ground, "I have told you, or told one of you Krampus kinder, we don't do Christmas."

"You do fairy tales. Christmas is a fairy tale. I am perfect for your agency."

"No, no, no. It sounds like ho, ho, ho, but it has more meaning. It means turn your furry legs around and get out of my fine establishment, why don't you. Christmas is not a fairy tale, it's a damned blight, is what it is. It does not tell a story, it creates a moral ethos through the wrappings of the fairy tale. The little man who goes down the chimney. The flying animals. But where is the story? It's just belief and that is not what we do in this place."

Krampus spread out his immense arms in a kind of surrender. "That is why I say I will be devil. Devil has no baggage like Christmas. I can do that job perfectly fine."

Ethel keeled over with sudden laughter. "Are you kidding me? The fairy tale of the devil is too messy for us to handle on a regular basis. One of the larger agencies handles the religious iconography. If you want to be hired out as a Devil or an Angel or as Jesus for that matter, you get in touch with the Blessed Talent Agency. They do that mishigoss as good as can be. You go there for that work."

Krampus lowered his head slightly, "I cannot. I have been there already and they say that they do not do Christmas. So much hatred is doled to the most wonderful time of the year."

"The most wonderful time of year is the fall when the World Series is happening, but I know what you are saying. The Blessed Agency and our little concern here do not want the potchke that Christmas hiring entails. "

Krampus seemed to get smaller. His shoulders hunched forward. He wrung his hands. "Oh, Ethel. Please. I am getting no work at the Jingle Jungle and I do not want to starve."

I couldn't help it. I needed to know, so I broke one of those rules Ethel likes to create and enforce upon me, and I interrupted her. "I'm sorry, but what is the Jingle Jungle?"

Ethel's face grew beet red and waggled a finger at me. Krampus was more even keeled. He turned to me and said, "Jingle Jungle is nickname for the agency that casts for Christmas archetypes."

"And now Easter," Ethel said. "They bought up the smaller agencies and now they own Easter, some of Halloween and all of Arbor Day, but they can have that one. Let them try to hire out trees and bushes for commercials."

"They are tough, unpleasant agency," Krampus added. "They are very strict and unpleasant. And they have now determined what is proper for Christmas and there has been a push to get rid of the fun, exciting parts of the season, namely the evil Krampus taking naughty children away. Why would they want to get rid of something so wholesome as Krampus?"

"Ya can't get work?" Ethel asked.

"Sadly, it is evident, there is no work in Christmas if it is Christmas with fangs."

"There should be fangs," Ethel said wistfully.

"There should always be fangs," Krampus gave out a hearty and mostly terrifying laugh. "I'm sorry to deceive, but I do need the work. There is nothing but homogenized images of the season. It is disgusting and hell on my bank account."

"That's the problem with a monopoly on a tale. The Jingle Jungle is the only place to get Christmas day players, and if that is the case, they call the shots on what can be seen. On what story is told. I hear they have even tried to get a foot in the Hanukkah market. Mashugunnah. They can have it. And what are they going to get? Walking, talking dreidels?" Ethel thought about it for a second a shivered.

"But where is the work for me? Even in a small agency like yours. Once I have Christmas on me, no will touch me. Am I blackballed because I am Krampus?" he asked.

"Pshaw kid. It ain't blackballing. That's too sophisticated for this gig. Don't blame us. The Jingle Jungle wants all Christmas and you know how greedy kids are when they think they deserve all the presents. Sorry. I wish you luck. Maybe Krampus will become popular again. Maybe there will be a redesign and you will be a cute cuddly kind hearted monster side kick to the Santa."

"That does not sound good to me. That sounds devilish in fact."

The Krampus left and Ethel whistled. "I feel for the guy. But Christmas is a racket, and everyone treats it like that. Once you are in the Christmas mob, you can never get out."

He came back a month later, claiming he was a troll ready ready and able to terrorize a billy goat gruff or two. Ethel didn't even let him through the door.

She said, "I'm sorry, pal. I like you. I like your spunk. But you got Christmas all up ya like a bad rash. We don't do Christmas. We wouldn't know how if we wanted to."

6. Huffing and Puffing

When it's very quiet at the agency, I get a sudden urge to be around people. Bea was always out drumming up opportunities. I hardly saw her. Ethel was the sister who was in the shop. Or she was supposed to be in the shop. Her office was empty a lot of the time.

So I had to get up and search for her. I am sure she must have thought me a noodge, but she was always kind in not telling me that to my face. When faced with a full day of balancing ledgers and issuing checks, it was nice to be around human contact. Contact that was happy to have me around. I didn't talk too much to Ethel and Bea, I just was needing to see them. If I didn't go out of my way to search for them, there was a good chance that I was going to be isolated.

I went out the back fire exit. It was my go-to search area. She was usually out back smoking. There she was, as good as caught. Ethel smoked in her office a lot of the time. When there was a commotion in the waiting area, she burst out past her door, a half burnt cigarette dangling off her bottom lip. She smoked in her office as she always had. But from time to time, Bea got pressure from the city and state to crack down on it and really meant it. This was one of those evangelical times. Times when Bea pestered her sister until she smoked out back.

Ethel did it without much under the breath mumbling. This time she was not alone. She was sharing the stoop with a large wolf wearing a tattered satin vest. He was smoking his gold tipped cigarette from a long tapered holder. "Tony," Ethel said, "have you finally come to your senses and are ready to ask for a drag." This was her typical question she gave me whenever I discovered her lighting up.

"Just getting some air. Enjoying the day."

"What air," The wolf asked, "the entire area is heavy with smoke. Like a nice Los Angeles smog."

"The company is nice," I said.

"Too right." The wolf said. "If you have to be alone and healthy or with people surrounded by carcinogens, it's' always best to pick the people. Be social but sickly, I always say." He slowly exhaled from his lungs and smoke slithered out like a web of a drunken spider.

"Uhm," I said looking at Ethel, asking permission for what I was about to say. Ethel, bless her, noticed the question in my hesitance and shrugged. "If you don't mind me asking, sir, but isn't smoking bad for, uhm, for an individual such as yourself."

The wolf dragged long on his cigarette. "The question you are asking is how is someone who makes a living huffing and puffing and blowing houses down, except for the ones that follow the code are constructed with brick. How can one such as that ruin his livelihood by smoking the foul weed. Tobacco. Not weed, weed. But I get you. How can I go down the path of emphysema and destroy my livelihood? Is that what you are asking?"

"Uhm." That was all I said.

Ethel ground out her cigarette. It made a good effect, but it was only because the cigarette was down to the filter. "Tony, don't insult one of our longest and best clients. Do you not think that he is professional enough? Tony, I know you are new, but a little decorum please. Really. People who don't smoke shouldn't be outside slumming with those that do." I don't know how she did it, but she gave me a yellow, ragged smile while saying that and I was not upset. The smile allowed her words to have no malice. Or, that's how I decided to think of it. She was still my boss.

The wolf laughed. "No need to scare the boy. He's about numbers and figures and that's an important factor in life, but it has nothing to do with art. I mean, the art that chooses someone. The thing about art, that moving finger, is that you still have to live. You need to have interactions and proclivities. You have to enjoy life, or it's not worth living. It's like blowing your mightiest at a brick building, to call up a useful metaphor."

"You give the blowing of the brick houses too much credit," Ethel said. "I always thought that was a stupid part of the story. The wolf should know better. The wolf is not an idiot. After seeing that it isn't working, why does he blow himself to exhaustion? All his other bad decisions, trying to go down the chimney. That was poor thinking brought on from exhaustion and oxygen deprivation from all that huffing and puffing."

"Yes," the Wolf nodded, "that is certainly true. There is a problem with the whole story. It always felt like two tales pushed together. You have the story of the marauding destruction against poor building practices. That can be seen as an interesting satire on work and sloth. But then the pigs are allowed to escape to house of their smarter brother. And instead of allowing the story to have it's logical moral, it becomes a castle keep situation with the crazed invader trying over and over to get in the house. How does that have anything to do with the moral of using better building products?"

"I thought the second part of the story showed how the smart planning of the third pig not only gave him a fine house, but also helped defeat the, uhm, the well, the enemy that is attacking."

"The huffing, puffing wolf you mean," the wolf clarified. "That's one way to see it, feels like padding to me. It does nothing for the narrative flow. And what kind of interior life can I, as a consummate and dedicated performer, create for such a cookie cutter, mustache twirling, antagonistic windbag? It is not a challenging or rewarding acting proposition.

"And because of that cartoon version with the music, that daft song about who is afraid, I am always dressed in only an oversized pair of rough hewn trousers attached to suspenders. I studied with some of the finest canine acting coaches on both coasts. My Iago was the best reviewed interpretation in any of the fairy tale Shakespearean productions. And they are having me in hobo pants and suspenders emote to a closed door that will not budge? It is too embarrassing, not to mention dull work."

"Come on sweety," Ethel said. "I think you are protesting too much, as one of your hoity toity characters might say. Three Little Pigs gigs pay the bills. Keep you in Merlot and cigarettes. You don't have to be artistically fulfilled with every call. You do these kind of roles because it frees you to have the financial wiggle room to do those plays you like that nobody ever goes to."

"And with that in mind, I take all the Red Riding Hood jobs you offer me. There is some meat on that role. It is a base villain, I am aware, and the directors are never interested in my suggestions, but at least I am not dealing with a dunder headed character. The scene in the woods asking what's in the bag. I can create some realistic tension with that."

"Oh, and you do," Ethel agreed. "Which reminds me, when you are doing Little Red in one of those preschool educational shows, could you just lower the sexual menace a little. All the directors are happy with your work, but are a little worried that you are performing for the parents more than the kids. Not a complaint, just a constructive note. I mean, I don't have a hard time booking you. Just something to consider."

"The performance I give is always a true and accurate portrayal of the inner being. Children will understand its truth. And you are talking about disturbing. That is the disturbing element to the tale? What about the cross dressing? What about the murder of the elderly? What about the cannibalism?"

I was aghast. "What? There is no cannibalism in Little Red Riding Hood."

The wolf laughed, "Of course there is. This is just another sign of the audience not being worthy of the source material."

Ethel lightly slapped the wolf. "Come now, don't be mean to the boy." She turned to me. "Tony, there are a lot of versions of the tale. If there wasn't, we wouldn't have a business here. There are several versions where the wolf puts the carcass of the grandmother on the sideboard, and then makes Little Red Riding Hood, eat some of the meat."

"Now that," the wolf stated. "That is acting. To convince a girl that the large hairy male in the bed is a little old woman and then to get her to eat of the flesh of the dead nanna. That's the ultimate of what we do. We teller of tales. We spinner of webs."

"You talker of garbage," Ethel added. "If you were willing to take Three Little Pig work, you would never be unemployed. There is always work for a versatile wolf. Pigs and grandmothers. That should be your bread and butter. I am happy to have such a good scary wolf for the Riding Hood. But just imagine if you weren't so limited."

"If I was more open minded, I would not be good at anything."

"Oh, that's just an excuse. It will allow you to look down on the huffers and puffers. It will give an excuse to kvetch that there ain't good work for such a lupin performer such as yourself. You should have all the work you can take, that would be such a crime?"

The wolf just chuckled and lit another gold tipped cigarette.

"Which reminds me, boychick. I got a call for a three little pigs wolf. Now wait. It's an anti smoking ad. The wolf has pulmonary issues and can't blow down a house of cards. What do you say."

"Of course. A part I was born to do." He dragged long and hard on the cigarette holder. "What a pleasure to be out here with you Ethel, and being allowed to say that I am practicing for my next great role."

7. Your Wishes Three

On Wednesday, Bea brought in Genies for an Aladdin production. There were very big burly men in the waiting area. There seemed to be a shortage of shirts because all of them were muscled and oiled down and completely bare chested. Most of them were bald, with a few sporting pigtails. Pointy shoes and baggy pants. It was all a lot of look.

Except for one. He wore a worsted suit.

I didn't know what a worsted suit was either, but he explained it to me. "It is when the wool is combed before spinning in order for the fibers to run in the same direction, But you do not need to know that information. You just need to know the finest suits are made this way. You see a supple, soft suit, you can be pretty sure it is worsted. Here. Feel it"

He pushed his arm in front of my face and would not remove it until I stroked it a few times. "Wow, that is smooth and soft. That really feels special."

"Of course," he said, "for I am special. I am the real kind of genie. An original."

I adjusted my glasses and gave him a serious looking at. He didn't look like a genie to me. Actually, he didn't look like a genie to anyone. He wasn't either tall or short. He was "guy" sized. Like if anyone asked how tall he was, I might shrug and state, "I don't know, he was as tall as a regular person."

He was sleek like his suit. Thin, but muscled. He stood poised in his leather shoes like a Russian ballet dancer, considering a sudden and perfect leap. He wore glasses, but you could tell that his eyesight was fine and he only wore glass lenses because he wanted to show off these gunmetal designer frames.

His skin was smooth and tanned. His eyes showed him to be Asian. His chin pointed slightly and he was so cleanly shaved, it might be easier to say that no whiskers ever dared to burst out from his face. His hair was dark and fine and neatly clipped.

I looked again and made up my mind, :Sure, you're a genie. Whatever. If you're a genie, I'm the Queen of Hearts."

In his hand appeared a deck of cards. I was pretty sure I didn't see him take the deck from a pocket. It was just there, in his hand. Great, now we had a sleight of hand magician. I put my hand on the pocket that held my wallet and kept it there, as a guard. He started shuffling the cards. There was a syncopated clicking as each card slid into its new position.

He shuffled seven times. Cut the deck a few more times. Tapped the top card with his index finger. The card flipped over on it's own, as if it was asked to introduce itself. The card was the Queen of Heart. The man's eyes bugged out in surprise, making sure that those in the cheap seats, a half mile away, could notice his wonder. "Oh. My. So this is you? Isn't it? Your highness."

"Nice trick."

"Thank you my good friend." He fanned out the deck and twisted his wrist, revealing to me that all of the cards were Queen of Hearts.

I couldn't help myself. I barked a laugh. He closed the deck and then fanned it open again. Now, all the cards were Jokers. It seemed apt. "Fine. I give up. You are a genie. You are the best genie in the world. There. Happy?" He nodded. "Still don't look like any genie I ever saw."

He closed the deck and tapped the top card. From the middle, a lone card wiggled up. It was a Jack of Clubs, but this was not like any normal Jack. It looked like a samurai, with top knot and sword. "Do I not look Middle Eastern enough for most discerning fairy tale tastes?"

I stared at the card. "Uhm. The genie is from Aladdin. Right?"

"That seems to be the current belief," the genie said while shuffling the deck.

"And Aladdin is from the Arrabian Nights stories. That mean it's Arabic. And geography was never my strong suit, neither was literature, but I think Arabic is the Middle East. So. Uhm. I kind of figured that the genie is Arabic. Or Muslim. Or Persian. Or something like that." I slapped my forehead with my palm. "I sound like an idiot."

"No." The cards shuffled. The top card flipped to reveal a typical genie. A big, brawny fellow with tawny skin and a cyclone of smoke where his legs should be. He looked like the other people in the waiting area, all the other genies vying for the job. "It's just people believe it to be. You are not an idiot, more than anyone else who consumes media information."

"Well. That's a relief?"

He laughed. "Perhaps so. The thing is, there is a wonderful text of tales. It was Persian, but then became an Arabic bestseller. Of course how many copies makes a bestseller when every copy is hand written? Twenty three? Two hundred and thirty seven? It doesn't matter, it was the rage for those who realized that the written word was a raging thing."

"I don't read that much."

"The Arabic version was translated in the eighteenth century by a French man. He included the story of Aladdin. It was not from the Persian or the Arabic iterations. It was a Chinese story." The top cards spun around on the rest of the deck like it was the base to an amusement park teacup ride.

"Chinese story," I said it to understand. "Oh. Oh. You are Asian. You are Chinese. You are an original."

The cards suddenly stopped spinning and the top card flew off the deck and landed in my hand. There was an ace of diamonds. The ace was a very Chinese lamp, the kind that might be in the lobby of a high end Chinese restaurant. The card showed a chinese boy, with top knot and round cherubic face rubbing the ace. From the top a genie appeared. It was a thin man who looked lot the man holding the deck of cards.

"Is any character in a fairy tale original? Isn't there any earlier version of me somewhere in an old Sumerian or Babylonian bestseller? The tale of Aladdin and the lamp can be as old as any culture who needed that story. Why they need the story, I am not quite sure. Why is this tale of wishes found and granted important? I stand in line in a convenience store behind all those instant scratch ticket jockeys and I must realize that I truly do not understand the nature of wishing and hoping."

"Wait," I said, handing the card back to him. The deck reached out at the wayward member and swallowed the ace of diamonds back into the fold. "What does the instant lottery have to do with you being a Chinese man in an Arabic story?"

"I guess it doesn't have much. I went off on a tangent. Like the story did. It jumped the cultural rails and went Chinese to Persian to Arabian to French pretending to be Arabian to Disney. Which is its own country of origin. Disney has its own borders and colorful passports. I was a debonair genie. I was closer to a traditional white haired ghost than anything Robin Williams performed in a cartoon. I was scary and uncertain, because getting your wish given to you is a frighteningly unbalanced event. It was a good story. It loses all of its subtlety and resolve in the version that is Middle Eastern with a thick French accent. The kind of aa accent mostly seen in cartoons with romantic skunks."

"Can you tell you me the original, I mean the earlier, Chinese version. You got me curious."

"I could. But I will not. You will not enjoy it. You will not listen to the story, but just compare it to the version you are familiar with. You will hold the two versions together and judge them like one of those puzzle magazine activities, where you have to spot the ten differences in the two purportedly identical pictures. You might find the story I am from interesting, but you will not find it a story you will get lost in."

The man walked back in the throng of other genies. Arab genies. Genies like I expect. He showed a few the genies his deck of cards and pulled out three cards face down.

Bea came out of her office and called out the name of one of the genies. She gave that genie, a big, broad bearded man with smoke for legs, a call card. The card had all the information for the upcoming gig. That was the prize. The call sheet. The one true winner. The genie thanked Bea and left with a smile. All the others moped through the door.

When they were all gone and the office was blessed with quiet, I said, "Bea, did you know that Aladdin was a Chinese story put into a French translation of the Arabian Nights stories. It was never part of the Arabian Nights. It's an imposter."

"What story isn't?" she shot back. She caught my surprised expression and smiled. "Yes, Tony. I was aware of that. Heard it from a well dressed Asian looking fellow who knows his way around a deck of cards."

I nodded. "He told you about too? Did he make it up?"

"Oh, no. I'm sure he's right. What guy makes up a story about him being a genie that no one will hire for an Aladdin job? He comes to every one of our open calls and he never gets the call card."

"Wait, he doesn't ever get hired? But he's a classical representation of the character."

"He might be more original than the other genies, but it's not what the audience thinks. You got to bow to the audience. They hear that there is an Aladdin story and when that lamp is rubbed they expect a muscled Middle Eastern fellow with a pointy beard. It might not be the right image, but it's the image they expect. He is a handsome Asian guy but he knows and I know that there is no way I can send him off on a job. It's not right, but we are helping stories be told. We might want to cast out of the box, but the people paying to see the show like the box. They want what they want. And what they want is the same version they already saw before."

I looked at the spreadsheet I was working on, to focus a little bit on things I understand. "Why does he come to the open calls if he knows he's not going to get called? He didn't strike me as a guy who would do something with no chance of winning."

"He's not here to win the role. He's here to fleece the other genies. He hangs around the waiting area and plays three card monty. He rakes it in. The other genies don't have sense enough to not play. For creatures of near infinite power, they are easy marks for a good card mechanic."

8. Ethel on the Phone

Philly, Philly. I hear you. Everyone in a fifty mile radius can hear you, with or without the phone. I hear you. You only want ogres. Big ugly ogres. Six of them. Ten? You want ten now. No. You didn't always say ten ogres. You said six ogres. Well I don't want to argue. Well, I want to argue a little bit, but not too much and not about the number of ogres I can't get you.

Did you hear that Philip, my dear? You might as well ask for seventy three ogres or three ogres, or two ogres and corgi puppy, because I can't get you any.

There are no ogres around. I have checked my book. Do you think I don't look at my book religiously? Yes, I have a book. I gave up on the rolodex. No. No computer. Isn't it good enough that I moved to a book?

But to go back to the main question. Who has ogres around? They left the business. They spent too long not getting any work, and went on to other things. Yes, there was a time that ogres were as popular as pet rocks and rubix cubes twenty years too late. Now with Shrek, the word ogre is back and big. If I can find one ogre, they want a mint, because they think they are the big commodity. Making it hard for a producer wanting some. You wanting five ogres right now, for example.

Yes, shotsi, you wanted ten. I was just hoping you came to your senses and settled on a reasonable number of flesh eating giants. I know. I know. Not giants. Ogres. I get it. This is not my first ogre rodeo you know.

But really Phil-bo, why can't you use giants. We can dress them with big ogre ears and ogre noses and who is the wiser. And the acting range on a giant? So much better than those monosyllabic ogres. I hook you up with a giant and you will have a Shakespeare spouting ogre.

I know. You don't need one. Heaven forbid you have a little class in one of your productions.

No giant? Okay. Then trolls, I'm up to my bellybuttons in trolls. Trolls look ogre-ish enough. Who's to say. Sure, they are gray and not green, but you have computers now, you can color them later on. It's like paint by numbers kits, you fill in the color you want afterwards.

Yes. I pick up the second phone and you can have twenty trolls at your set in an hour. No, would I exaggerate? I wouldn't even know how.

Well, it's because they all suddenly lost their regular jobs and are desperate for work. Don't tell them that, don't let them know that we know they are desperate. Anyway, you can get them for a song. A tune. You can whistle three random notes and you will have them. They will be the best ogres you have ever seen. Outside of real ogres.

Only you, me and their therapist will need to know they are trolls. I'm not selling you fake goods. This is not a Louis Vuitton handbag with misspellings on the nameplate.This is just a way to get someone before the camera. Why worry that they are trolls. The audience will love them. They can be pretty scary.

There's a reason Phil. They ain't bad boys. They ain't lousy performers. No. There's a reason. A bunch of them got sick of the up and downs of show business. They loved me. Of course they loved me. Who doesn't have a flame for Ethel? Don't answer that. The answer is no one. Just to make sure we are all clear. But they got sick of them all going for a roll, a Billy Goats Gruff gig and there was only one part. The work was sparse.

So they got together and left the business. Yes. As one. They are all very cliquey. Maybe they are a tribe. So that would mean they are very tribey. And the head of the group decided they were going to get mundane consistent employment. I know. It hurts my tongue to utter such poison.

But that's what they did. They left as a group and got into the best troll job ever. They worked as toll gate attendants. Yeah. The people giving out tickets and getting toll money. They worked mostly bridge tolls, but you couldn't always guarantee that, so they were magnanimous and did the Thruway, the Mass Pike and whatever road that needed the folks driving on it to be shaken down. Cleaned of all coins.

Yes, Phil. Yes. Chances are good that if you had a surly toll worker, it was a troll. They weren't paid for being mean and rude to the drivers, that was just an added bonus. A flourish of the trade.

No, they didn't change the way they looked. They looked like trolls. It would be a major insult if they were asked to hide their appearance. Trolls are not a proud race, but they hate wearing makeup. Even eyeliner.

They were all perfect toll workers. They caused major back up and made everyone ashamed for not bringing exact change. Oh, and the fun they'd have when some poor son of a bitch lost their toll ticket. They made the drivers regret being in a car that day. They terrorized the motorists, which is what the toll worker is meant to do.

But all things have to end. You got it, the electronic toll systems. The transit authority found something more terrifying than trolls in toll booths, automatic billing. More frightening than any of my lovely trolls.

Which is why they are available. And they're hungry for it. Not just for goats, though throwing in a few billy goats gruff on the catering table would not be such a bad idea. It would show them they were appreciated.

Come on Phil, my love, my open minded fellow. Trolls are the next big thing. You will look back at this moment, this conversation and thank all those that need to be thanked for listening to your Ethel on this day. People will point to this moment when the boring preponderance of ogres in mass media finally ended. And it will be you, you did it. You listened and the world is better and more trollish because of it.

So what will it be, Philly Cheese Steak? Should I send you the full ten? You can have them at your door in two hours. They move fast. Yes. I can see that might be too much. Four? How about four? And a giant with makeup on? So five of my best. That we can do. Good choice.

9. Just Right

April robs me of sleep. Ask anyone who works the ledger and then files with the government will know. April is a mean month that pokes me awake in the middle of the night to remind me that I forgot two forms and that it can't wait until the morning. In the back of my dreamless brain, I know it can wait until the morning, or even the next afternoon. I know this all, but then April plays with my thinking and I am out of bed and heading into the office. There is that poem that starts with the line "April in the cruelest month." I am in complete agreement, but for a different reason than what the poet probably was thinking of.

And that was why I roused out of my bed at eleven PM on a Friday night and biked over to the employment office. A dispersal form was nagging at me and I knew it was going to pester me the entire weekend if I didn't do something about it immediately. I was expecting a dark storefront, but there was a light on at the back, coming from the conference room. I never had seen anyone go into that room, there was never a need for a conference as far as i noticed. But that was where the light came from.

The door was unlocked. I pushed it half open and craned my head in, "Hello, is anyone there?"

A voice from the back shouted, "Is that the Chinese food, bring it over and we will see what we have for money. Just kidding, I'm charging the business."

I walked toward the light, "It's no food, it's Tony."

Ethel walked out of the room. All I could see was a silhouette, but I knew it was her. From the strong whiff of old tobacco. "Tony, I know I instill loyalty in everyone I work with, but bubbula,I ain't paying you for working late on a Friday You should be out. Doing things that are not here."

I headed to my desk and turned on my light. "I know. I'm crazy. I have to correct this mistake on our filings tonight or I will not be able to enjoy the weekend."

"Who am I to stop anyone from working on my behalf for no extra money. Let me say that again, because I like the sound of my own voice, no extra money. And if the guy from Panda Pagoda comes, can you pay for it, and I'll get you next pay period. There's a boy."

I opened up the spreadsheet and checked the tax law cheat sheet I made up and got to work. There was a lot of shouting and swearing and clicking. Like someone was tap dancing in high heels. I was distracted, not sure what that sound was, but I was soon focused on the problem. Yes, indeed. There was most definitely a problem and we were going to get creamed if I didn't go back and fix a line on almost every form. I didn't pause, I just got down to the work of it.

"Working hard, ain't you."

I jumped.

That was said right next to me, in a small but determined voice. My heart was in my throat and I was practically on the ceiling.

"I guess I startled you."

I almost jumped again. I know there was someone in the room next to me, but there was something alarming about the voice speaking again. Wasn't once bad enough?

I turned to my right and saw a little girl in a hoodie. Not a red riding hood. A sweatshirt, with a hood, with the word "sassy" written on the front. Blonde tresses peaked out of the hood. Her nose was button like and she would have been as cute as the dickens if she didn't have an old, tired look in her eyes. "I've been in the waiting area the whole time you've been here. I was ten feet from you for forty minutes and you never noticed me. I'm sorry for saying this, but what the hell is wrong with you? Is work so engrossing?"

I thought about it. I had an answer, but I didn't like it. I thought on it for a little longer and decided to tell the truth. "Yes. Yes it is that engrossing. I trust in numbers. They tell a story that I understand. Their equations and set rules are better than any Once Upon a Time tale we cast for. I understand numbers and actions. It makes me feel justified. It makes me the storyteller."

The gurl snorted out a fast laugh. "That is so stupid. Two Pi R is not a story, it's a way of looking at a circle. A circle is where you sit and tell a story, it isn't the story itself."

"What are you doing here, isn't it past your bedtime?" I asked in my haughtiest tone.

"You wish." She was about to go back to the waiting area, but she stopped and turned back to me. "The old woman who I look after is in the back, losing more of her savings to Ethel and the other mahjong hustlers."

There was a lot to unpack in that statement, but what I asked was, "What's mahjong?"

"It's a tile based game originating in China. Little old ladies from certain neighborhoods of Brooklyn seem to love it. As the little old ladies have moved from their brownstones, so has mahjong. Not a lot of people play it anymore. This might be the only weekly game on this coast. Ethel likes to hustle everyone. She used to run a bridge game, but she was blatantly cheating and the other girls got sick of it. They figure that if she is cheating, she should do it with more panache."

"Is she cheating with this mahjong?"

"Oh, sure, though no one knows exactly how. That's part of the fun."

I stared at her face, she looked familiar. "You have gone on castings with us, right? I've seen you here before. Right?"

"I get a good call rate. I usually don't have to come in. Ethel has me on speed dial."

"Ah," I said, "you are just showing off."

"If you say so."

"If Ethel cheats," I asked, "why do you let your grandmother play every week."

The girl started to answer the question and then noticed something in what I said, stopped, and began to laugh hysterically. "You think she's my grandmother? That's good."

"Sorry, it just seemed logical."

"That's good too. That's even better. You are working here and looking for logic." She threw back her head and laughed so hard, the hood fell off and a tangle of blonde tresses fell down over her shoulders.

She stopped laughing and I knew who she was. "You're Goldilocks!"

"You are such a smart fellow. So bright. Like a bag full of smashed light bulbs. I sure hope you are better with numbers than you are with recognizing literary archetypes."

"And the woman is not your mother, or your aunt? I mean the story doesn't mention Goldilocks's family. But everyone has a family."

The color in the young girl's face drained and any vestige of the laughter was completely gone. "Archetypes. We are archetypes. Red Riding Hood has a mother that sends her off to her doom. She is not a mother, she is a change agent. She is a catalyst. She is the hinge in the door that opens and lets the story begin. Same thing with the parents in Hansel and Gretel. Their purpose is to remind us that grown ups are right bastards. Adults would rather eat and have sex then raise children. The old woman I am with is not an agent of change. She has been changed. Into me, but she is not a catalyst. She is what the catalyst reacted upon. Stop gawping at me, the old woman is an earlier Goldilocks."

I thought about this. "I didn't know you could age, could get old. Stands to reason. Not a lot of call for an octogenarian Goldilocks, though. I guess if there is some medication they want advertised for the elderly that they might use an old Goldilocks for. This laxative is too hard. This laxative is too soft. That kind of thing."

"She's not an aged Goldilocks. She is the original Goldilocks. Though, not with that name."

"Wait," I said with confidence, "I understand. There is no way to say the original version because fairy tale characters have no beginning. There is no one first version of a character, they are all iterations. They mutate like viruses. See. Four months here I think I am finally getting it."

"Yes," the girl said, now with a little red in her cheeks from anger. "You have learned a lot about archetypes and repetitive tropes, but with me, and the woman I am with, you are totally wrong. She is the original."

"Yeah. I give up. I will stick to numbers from now on."

"The thing is. The part that is hard to understand is that you are right, these stories that we tell and retell are like a virus. But a virus that instructs and entertains. As we change, the virus story changes, keeping its potency up. They teach us to be wary of men or wolves in the woods. Not to eat ourselves stupid, no matter how hungry we might be. And they change and stay the same, for the most part. And the stories are built on the stories of the past. No one is the author because a thousand tongues and million listening ears were involved in the construction of just one of those stories.

"But the Tale of the Three Bears is not a fairy tale. It is a piece of literature created by one author. We even know who that was. Some British guy named Robert Southey. The same year that he wrote it, someone made a verse version of it. The same year and it was already getting covered like it was fodder for a bar band. This was the first one hit wonder.

"The story didn't have a young cherubic girl with blonde curls. The agitator coming into the unguarded house was an old homeless woman. She was ugly and ragged. She was nobody's hero. When the bears came back, she jumped out the window and then the narrator stated that no one knows what happened to the old woman, she could have been arrested and put into prison or she could be dead. That's how the story ended. But we know what happened to her, you and I. She turned up playing mahjong, and losing money at a painful rate.

"The story was good enough to want to retell, but not good enough with the old woman in the center. She quickly changed into a cutesy pie girl. But I got to say, this is not a fairy tale. This is a cuckoo's egg left in the nest of Mother Goose."

I stared at her for a few moments and said, "You don't talk like a little girl, you know that?"

"Because I'm not. I am almost as old as the woman slamming tiles back there. I am only as young as an editorial suggestion, hey why don't you make the woman a sweet girl. The story will go down so much smoother that way. It will not be as mean. And maybe we shouldn't mention that we hope the woman is dead or imprisoned. Let's just leave it to the audience's imagination. If they even have one anymore. I am the cosmetic alteration. The gene splice to a palatable criminal."

"Goldilocks is not a criminal, she is the heroine of a fairy tale."

"I sure hope you are good with numbers," she said with a rueful laugh. "The woman or the girl or the whatever of the story is nothing but a criminal. She is a terrible monster. She breaks in. She eats their food. She breaks their furniture. She squats in the bed. She's just a dumb old or dumb young female who doesn't know not to fall asleep because the owners are probably coming back. Bad planning. And the rightful residents return and they are not monsters. They can be bears or just angry citizens upset that their house was vandalized and no one was going to do anything about it.

"You know the text doesn't say that Humpty Dumpty is an egg. But the text doesn't say that Goldilocks is a larceny queen. Think of the crappy things this cherubic little doll does? And at the end she always finds the just right version. The text doesn't say she is being good and sweet. The text just says that she she got some grub and busted out of there without a second to spare."

"Okay, you are Goldilocks and she is Goldilocks. I get it."

"No, not really. You don't. I am Goldilocks. And she is the old lady who used to live in the story. She doesn't live there anymore because cute pushed out the cuckoo from the nest. That old woman didn't have a name and she still doesn't. She's just an old lady I feel bad for. I make sure she doesn't lose more money than she can afford to give to Ethel. I make sure she doesn't drink so much that she winds up passed out in the background of a Princess and Frog retelling."

"You're a good friend."

"No. I'm a sore winner." Her adorable nose scrunched up like she was smelling delicious cookies burning in the oven. "I keep her around because I am hoping that tastes will change. That people will suddenly desire authentic tales. And I will be pushed aside for the original. The one who made it the first time. I am hoping that she will take over again and leave me to my own devices."

I thought I got it. "You want to be free of the bears and the house and the porridge. Free of the groupings of three and the beds and the just rights. You want a story that." I ran out of what I was about to say. I am a person of ledgers and numbers and canceled checks, I was doing pretty good having original thoughts so late at night, but the wall of reasonable assertions slammed into me and I exhaled out all the whimsy.

"You're close, close enough. I want to be in a story that doesn't end with me jumping out a window and mad dashing it out of there. I am tired of being more hair style than girl. I am just tired. And I wasn't even supposed to be the character."

"Will that happen?" I asked.

"Will the older me ever win at mahjong?" the young girl asked back.

Just then, there was a rowdy whooping sound from the back room. It had to be Ethel. It had to be her winning. I didn't need that to know what the answer to the girl's question was. The laughter of winning and the silence of those who lost was just a nice exclamation to the story. The final line that means the end, and they all lived happily ever after.

10.Ethel on the Phone

I know how you feel. I know how you feel deep down in my bones, Reuven. There are no good names anymore. I hear you. For all I know, I am the last remaining Ethel in existence. And where are the Avrams? The Haimis? The Schlomos? I don't know the last Pinchas I ever ran into. Oh wait, stop, I do know the last Pinchas. He was a gonif who hitched his wagon to a pretty schiktsa I used to book as Snow White. Snow White? Snow white bread was what she was. How she got married to a Pinchas I do not have an inkling. I had to cut ties with the girl because Pinchas weaseled money out of me. Money he swore his wife was to earn for me sometime down the line. How did I get hoodwinked by such a shnook? Maybe it was the Pinchas factor. I just wanted to trust such a name, I didn't think of the person attached to it. I am still hoping to find another real named person. I will even kvell if there I meet another Pinchas. I will not lend him a penny, but I will be pleased to call him by his name. Not a penny to give, remember that.

So of course it makes me sad that you want to be called Ronny. That is not a name, it is the way you order eggs, over easy and Ronny. You are not eggs Reuven, you have a fine brave name. I know you might not see it that way, but it is true all the same. You got to say that yes, I am Reuven Stiltstein and I make a living pretending to be an evil man who makes dreadful bargains and can spin gold from straw. This is just an aspect of yourself, it is how you make a living. That can come and go. But your name? Your real name, that is not a jacket you hang up in the closet and wait for it to come back into style again.

You got yourself a name Ellis Island and all the picture book adaptations couldn't take away. Sure, sure. They don't know you as Stiltstein. I know what they call you. I've booked you for over a 100 Rumple gigs over the years. I should know what they call you. You always get the bookings. Everyone knows what the original is and why that's the best. Stop it Reuven, you are the best evil gnome creature who lives in the woods and makes impossible bargains for babies. Simply the best.

Yes, dear of course its anti-semitic. Did this just occur to you? Did you suddenly realize that the giant nose and the money lust and the crazed endlessly long name is a stand in for a nice Jewish fellow trying to make a living?

It doesn't matter. Most people don't realize it either. So if no one knows its offensively anti-semitic does it stay anti-semitic? The answer, of course, is yes. You don't need a critic to tell you that something is bad, just like old milk still stinks even if your nose is stuffed up with a cold.

No. You're right. I don't want you to stop doing it. Anti-semitic or not, derivative or not, boring and obvious as any wives tale or not. It's a good living for you and it sure makes me a winner in the eyes of any casting agent. I mean, you kill it. They say to me, they say Ethel, I know there are tons of Rumples to choose from, but there was this one Rumple more disgusting than all the others, that's the one I want. The vilest one. No dear, that is the complement.

To my mind, the Rumple is the hero of the piece. The girl who became queen and the king are vile monsters. You just have to look at it the right way. You are the hero of the piece. My hero always, Reuven.

That's why changing your name is such a blow, even if no one watching the story knows. You just can't do it. You have to have the name that you believe in. In the story, the schlamazel Rumple believes in his name so much that it can give up all his well earned wealth. It is so powerful that he has to give it all. Think of that when someone calls you Ronny.

You ain't going to be more popular and you will still only get the Rumple roles. It's just the way it turns out. But if you want to do some gnome work, or be a goblin, I can hook you up, but you are too proud. You told me so. You said you are too proud to take that kind of work. So take the job you hate and change your name to feel better? But I will know who are, boychik. I will know how good you can be. And besides, I have a jewelry store commercial set up for next week, you game? Whatever your name is?

11.The Origin of Stories

Near the end of the day, I wandered back and heard a few people talking and laughing. When I went out to find out who was there in the day's cigarette mob, It was Ethel and three dwarfs we recently hired out for a Snow White film. I was shocked to see Bea in the corner, trying to avoid the lingering smoke.

They saw me, gave me a nod and went back to the conversation. The tallest dwarf said, "Now, it's like I was telling you. This was not for kids. This was weird meta fiction that made no sense to me."

The second tallest dwarf raspberried him, "Come on, who cares if it is for kids or grad students. We had a gig, we knocked it out of the park. It's what we do."

"Yeah," the tallest dwarf said. "Sure. Work is work. And God bless it. But come on, the whole thing with the gardener was weird, right?"

"I wasn't paying attention," the third tallest dwarf said. "I was learning my lines and trying to understand my motivation. That takes concentration, you know."

Ethel cackled, "What the hell are you talking about, motivation? Your character likes tall chicks. That's it. End scene."

The tallest dwarf nodded and said, "The gardener was a new character for this film. He comes to the evil stepmother and offers to sell her a magical apple."

"That's not how the story goes," the second tallest dwarf pointed out. "The story is that the evil stepmother created the poisonous apple. That's part of it and call me a traditionalist, I want the stories to be what they have always been."

The tallest dwarf winked at me, "This is what I have to put up with all day. Up to here, I put up with it. Listen, I don't care if this is the same story or a complete overhaul, the gardener in this flick was weird."

"What was the gardener about?" Bea asked.

"Thank you Bea. A real question, and not an annoyed question. We were not in this scene, but it ran to multiple takes and creeped into the scene we were in, so it just happened that we saw a few takes. A random guy comes in and offers to sell her this apple that will do what she needs it to. The queen has no idea who he is or how he knows she wants to poison Snow White. The queen don't like it that there is someone who knows her plans and there is plenty scenery eating going on."

"You should talk, Mr. Histrionics," the third tallest dwarf said.

"The gardener is all dirty and ruined. He held up the apple. He said that it was an ancient relic, something he has kept all these years. He said that he was a gardener where two naked people lived. He goes on describing this garden he worked at and it doesn't take much to figure out that he is describing the Garden of Eden."

"I didn't get it," the third tallest dwarf said. "You had to tell me it was the Garden of Eden. And I'm still not convinced."

"And we are judging the level of intelligence for the audience by you? For you, it's a Biblical miracle when you wear your pants the right direction. They don't need to say that it was an apple from the Tree of the Knowledge of Good and Evil for the smart folk in the theaters to figure out that that is what it is."

" I like that idea," Bea said. "This production got an interesting angle. It brings in a lot of texture and nuance by throwing in the Book of Genesis. A cool angle. But is it their angle?"

"What do you mean?" Ethel asked.

"I have a feeling I have seen that before. The melding of the Garden of Eden myth with the Snow White folktale. I want to say that it's been done."

"I felt the same way!" the tallest dwarf shouted. He was so loud the second tallest dwarf and Ethel jumped two feet back. I might have moved back myself a little.. "I thought that too and I said that to the producer. I introduced myself and asked him, hey pal, did the Garden of Eden gag come from someplace?""

"You asked the producer of the show if he stole an idea from someone else? What the hell, Tommy?" Ethel shouted. Now it was Bea's turn to jump back from the sudden explosion of yelling. "What are you, an idiot? I don't hire dumb dwarfs. I expect you all to be short, sure, but you have to have a little bit of common sense!"

"Don't worry one bit about that, Ethel. The guy seemed to be alright with that. He laughed and said he thought so too when he first read the script. He talked to the screenwriter, asking him if he came up with that idea or if it was from someone else. So he ain't going to call you guys here to complain about me, he was fine with it."

"Yeah, he was fine to your face, but I bet you your next two paychecks that I am going to get a call from him sometime tonight. And I am sure he was not alright with the hired help wondering if his movie plagiarized another story. Yeah. For sure, a phone call. At least."

"Maybe," Bea said. "Maybe this was the first time this neat idea occurred but it should have been around for a long time prior. Maybe this story concept was shy or lazy or both and only came out now, though it should have been already out there. Stories are like that. If they appear before their time, they are ignored and ridiculed. If they come around after they should have, then we get a sense that we have heard it before. That it is not original. It is original because someone should have hatched that idea thirty years ago and didn't, so now it's stuck being a case of first run deja vu. Well, you know what I mean."

Ethel shook her head, "Not one bit."

The tallest dwarf said, "I know what she means. She means that it could be an original idea or it could be something stolen and reused, but the important part is that we question the validity of the parts of the story. We have to understand that the fairy tale is like a Frankenstein Monster and the parts are sewn together into a gestalt."

"That's not what I mean," Bea said, "I don't know if that is anything but a drunken cry for help."

"And we should do now, what I always do when I stumble on a cry for help," Ethel said. "And that is turn up the music real loud and act like no one else is there."

The second tallest dwarf piped in, "Well I don't care if the story came from an old housewife in Germany or in the Book of Genesis, as long as there is work and that I can get hired to that work, then that's all that matters. The story can come from the phone book for all it matters to me."

"Amen to that. The Origin of stories is one thing," Ethel said, "but being able to tell that tale is the money. You can have the cleverest variation on a theme, but if no one is there to watch it, then it's an interesting theory and not a ripping yarn."

"Stories be stories," the third tallest dwarf said and we all left it at that.

12.Work Review on a Mattress

I was finishing up for the week, Friday night was beckoning to me. A big Friday night, for me, was take-out Chinese and maybe something loud and violent to watch on the TV. The waiting area smelled of bad cigars, due to the Old King Cole casting call we had earlier. King Cole castings were the worst. Not only did they stink up to high heaven, they were so big we could only accommodate six or seven of them at a time. Which caused us to stagger King Coles all day. They sure did stink. And they were constantly ordering me around, or at least trying to. I spent the morning staring at a spreadsheet I had already taken care of. I had to look at something.

The door was open and I had the fan blowing out into the street. It was getting better as I went for my coat. I was zipping up when the door to Ethel's office slammed open. I was shocked to see both of the sisters try to get out of the space at once. With some shoving and pushing, Ethel came out first. Big surprise.

"Alright, Boychik, it's been six months you have worked for us. I told you to give us six months."

"Six months was four months ago," I pointed out.

She swished her hand in front of me. The act made her lose her balance a little bit, and I figured she had her end of the day tipple a little early. "Close enough. What's four months between friends?"

"Well employee and employer, not really friends," Bea clarified.

Ethel winced, "No, of course, not friends. Never friends. I'm lucky to know his name."

"Tony," I said helpfully.

"This is why we are not friends. He still doesn't know when I am in the middle of a long winded monologue. How has he been here for five months and not know that you don't interrupt Ethel when she is going full steam a head?"

"Ten months," I said again. I know I should have been quiet. But she was making mistakes with numbers and that was something I could not ignore, even if it was not the prudent thing to do.

Bea tsked both of us. "It doesn't matter if you have been here for five or six or ten years. It doesn't matter if you are a friend or an underling. Just so you know Tony, I don't think of you as an underling, that's Ethel's word for you."

"Only when I don't agree with his accounts. We should be taking in a lot more money than that. Only an underling can get it that wrong. He should be happy I say that and not call him a gonif."

"But we wouldn't call him that, because Tony is not a gonif and you are just being too Ethel for typical normal consumption. But as I was saying. It matters not at all what we call you, the truth is that we need to figure out what to do with you. Ethel gave you six months to decide if you liked it here and if we liked you, and maybe we missed the mark by a season or two, but here we are. With your employment review."

"And I got the mattresses in the back room to make it official," Ethel said.

This scared me more than anything I ever came across while working there. They were going to put me to the mattresses? I came up with a few scenarios of what it could mean, and I was not pleased with any of them. "How bout you give me a written summary of my work and we can go from there. I can reply in writing as well. Nothing better than a good clean neat legal paper trail."

Ethel turned to Bea, "What's he talking about? What is that crazy kid saying?"

"Well it can be two things, I think," Bea said back. "He heard mattresses and thought we were going to reenact the Godfather and go to the mattresses."

"I never saw that movie. I don't do scary human movies, you know that Bea."

"Sure I do, but sometimes I want to prove that I know more than you. Even if its an old gangster flick. Going to the mattresses in that genre translates going to war with another gang. I guess he could think we are bringing out the tommy guns and going to strafe Lange and Sons Employment and Casting."

"Serves those momsers right, but we ain't going to shoot them, too many witnesses," Ethel said.

"The other thing it could be is that he thought we were going to bring him to the mattresses and do what some people like to do on mattresses."

"Wait," Ethel said, slamming her hand down. "Is that what he thought? Is that what he thinks of us and mattresses? If I wanted to do anything with that undernourished body of his, I wouldn't waste on one of our mattresses. That's why God created the casting couch. Not a mattress."

Bea sighed and looked at me. "This is just Ethel being Ethel. She would never disrespect anyone working here. She's just trying to be funny and failing once more."

"You just don't have a funny bone in you, sister dear."

"The part you didn't figure out, Tony, is that there is option three."

"What's option three?" I asked.

Ethel spit, she looked annoyed. Well, she looked like Ethel, but just more so. "Come to the back office and see. Why are we talking? We have a review to do."

We walked to the back and I got my first glimpse of fifteen or eighteen mattresses stacked one on top of the other.

"When you said mattresses," I said in a low wondering tone, "you meant mattresses."

"This is how it goes here at Madre and Gander. When we find an employee that makes it past the initial probationary period," Ethel explained, "they come across this compatibility test."

"How many people have made it pass the probationary period," I asked.

"Well, uh, the probationary period is really tough," Ethel said quickly, "who can say where the good employees are. Anyway. What we do, or will do, is to place you on the top mattress and you have to feel the items we placed in the bottom mattresses. Now the girls of the story insist that it be a pea. A pea. No way am I going to use a pea that will stain the mattress, and where will my security deposit be? Gone, that's where it will be. No, we place helpful things for the work we do here and you must identify them just by lying on the mattress. A snap. It will be such a snap."

"What do I get if I can identify them?" I asked.

"The more you get," Ethel said, "the more your raise will be."

"What happens if I get none of them right?"

The sister looked at each. Their mouths dropped open. Bea started to speak and then shrugged. Ethel sighed. "Why bother with such outliers. Such points of unnecessariness? Why do you have to think of things that are impossible? Like those poor Ali Babas we get coming in They have to make the magic rug fly by not thinking of the word "elephant." You can't not think of elephant once I tell you to not think of elephant. Same thing here. How can you fail if you think of the word fail. Just lie on the damned mattresses and we can get going with talking about bonuses and pay raises. The stuff you will like to hear and make my blood freeze. I hate paying money, but you, boychik, I can thaw slightly for."

I looked at the mattresses. I took in Ethel and then Bea. I looked at the mattresses once more and then craned my neck to see my desk. It was clean and ordered. I had a small picture frame on my computer. I left it blank. I knew who I dreamed of being in there. I didn't need to share it with anyone. I looked at it and imagined who should be in there and was happy. She always had a beautiful smile on, a different smile for every time I glanced at the frame.

I looked at the sisters and said, "I will stay on. I will take whatever raise you have for me. But I'm not going on the mattresses. So if I get a smaller raise, that's fine with me."

"Why," Ethel asked, "afraid of heights?"

I laughed. "No. I just want to do it this way. Well, I'd rather not be part of any story. I just want to keep the books. Generate the checks, make sure the stories go forward. I just don't want any story for me. The mattresses? They are too much story for my liking. It makes me nervous. Just let me continue working and being in the background. Is that okay?"

Bea and Ethel smiled. I think they even teared up. I don't know why, but that what it looked like. "I guess that will be fine," Bea said.

"You would have aced it, and the raise you would have been swimming in," Ethel added.

"And," Bea went on, "that doesn't matter at all. You do what you want. We're lucky to have you here Tony." She brought out her hand and I shook it. I was happy to do that.

They talked about the money and the benefits and they were fine. More than fine. The only thing, Ethel seemed annoyed. "What's wrong?" I asked her around closing time.

She said, "Looks like it's me that has to get rid of the mattresses. Next time, when I have a great idea, I should do the world the favor of not doing anything with it."

About the Book

Fairy tale movies and commercials are everywhere. They are very popular. And that's great, because all those fairy tale characters need the work. All the Snow Whites, Three Pigs and a variety of Big Bad Wolves all are clients of the Madre and Gander Employment Agency. That's how Humpty Dumpty finally gets a crack into Show Business.

Madre and Gander is a casting agency where they supply all the fairy tale denizens a film production can ask for. Ethel and Bea own the agency and they have their hands filled dealing with all the temperamental folkloric archetypes.

You will discover the Rapunzel that shaved off her hair. There is Krampus trying to be a troll to get more work. Also, you will read of the two different types of Goldilocks living together. From asthmatic Wolves, to a job performance review that entails a pea and a crap load of mattresses.

If you want to see fairy tales in a very different manner, then grab an application and sign up as a client for Madre and Gander, employment agency to the fairy tales.

About the Author

David Macpherson was inspired to write this book after finishing John Kendrick Bangs's story collection, Jack and the Check Book. It was published over a hundred years ago and it was the spark to write this book. To be fair, David didn't like Jack and the Check Book. He likes the author, but not that book so much. So instead of writing a nasty review of it on Good Reads, he wrote an entire book of his own. And that's what you have in your hands now. David has written a bunch of other things you might like. Check him out at all the sites that sell ebooks. You can also see his antiquated blog at 100pagedash.wordpress.com.